Dear Master Dragon

~ a Comic Coloring Book Story ~

by Alva Sachs

illustrated by Patricia Krebs

For Kaylie~
Dream Big!
Alva Sachs

Three Wishes
Publishing Company

Dear Master Dragon

Signature Book Printing– www.sbpbooks.com – Printed in the United States.

Illustrations and graphic design by Patricia Krebs.

Editor: Cheri Dellelo– www.dellelo.com

First edition published in 2013 by Three Wishes Publishing Company

26500 West Agoura Road, Suite 102–754
Calabasas, CA 91302
Office: 818–878–0902
Fax: 818–878–1805
www.threewishespublishing.com

Library of Congress Cataloging–in–Publication Data:

Sachs, Alva.
Dear Master Dragon by Alva Sachs; illustrated by Patricia Krebs. –– 1st ed.
p. cm.
SUMMARY: Danny Dragon decides to write a letter to the Master Dragon for help.
Why would Danny need help? Will the Master Dragon write him back, or will he have to solve his problems by himself?
Join Danny on his adventure as he discovers what it is like to be a real dragon.

Audience: Ages 3–8

LCCN: 2013946226
ISBN–13: 9780979638039
ISBN–10: 0979638038

1. Dragons–– Juvenile fiction. [1. Dragons––Fiction.]
I. Krebs, Patricia, 1976– illustrator. II. Title.

PZ7.S11852Dea 2013 [E]
QBI13–600125

For children everywhere who enrich the world with their imaginations and inspire me to write.

GIVING ONE LAST LOOK AROUND, DANNY QUICKLY RAN TO THE MAILBOX, AND SLIPPED HIS LETTER INTO THE SLOT.

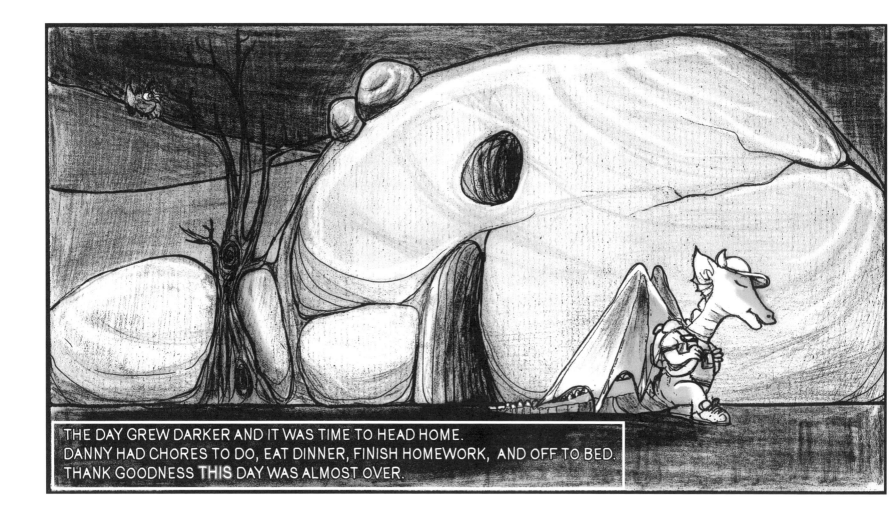

THE DAY GREW DARKER AND IT WAS TIME TO HEAD HOME.
DANNY HAD CHORES TO DO, EAT DINNER, FINISH HOMEWORK, AND OFF TO BED.
THANK GOODNESS **THIS** DAY WAS ALMOST OVER.

THE NEXT MORNING, DANNY THOUGHT...

HE QUICKLY ATE HIS BREAKFAST,
GATHERED HIS SCHOOL STUFF,
AND HUGGED HIS DAD AND MOM GOODBYE.

TODAY
will be different.

TRYING TO PICK HIMSELF UP FROM THE GROUND, HE SAW SHADOWS OF OTHER DRAGONS ALL AROUND HIM.

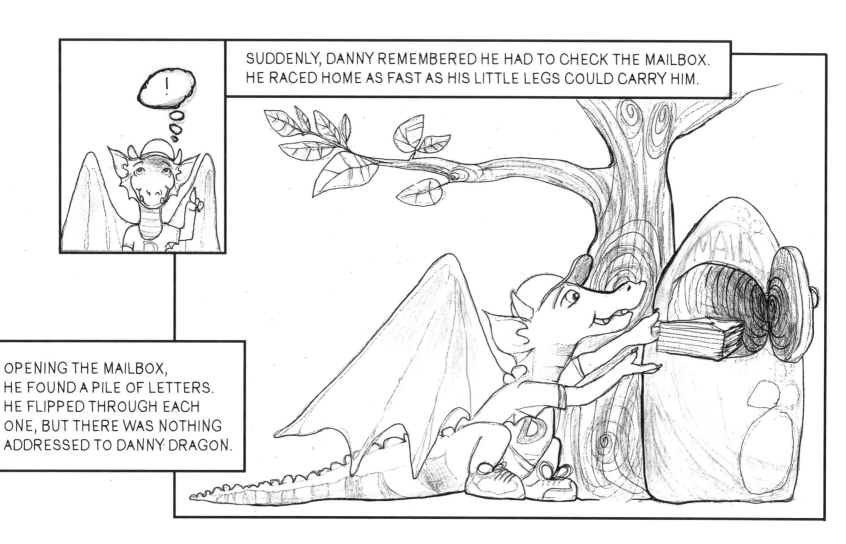

SUDDENLY, DANNY REMEMBERED HE HAD TO CHECK THE MAILBOX. HE RACED HOME AS FAST AS HIS LITTLE LEGS COULD CARRY HIM.

OPENING THE MAILBOX, HE FOUND A PILE OF LETTERS. HE FLIPPED THROUGH EACH ONE, BUT THERE WAS NOTHING ADDRESSED TO DANNY DRAGON.

EVERY DAY AFTER SCHOOL, DANNY AND DINA WOULD MEET AT THE PARK UNDER THE OAK TREE.
CLIMBING TO THE HIGHEST BRANCH, DANNY TOOK A DEEP BREATH, CLOSED HIS EYES,
AND WAITED FOR DINA TO COUNT TO THREE.

ONE...

TWO...

THREE!

DANNY JUST STOOD THERE FROZEN ON THE BRANCH.

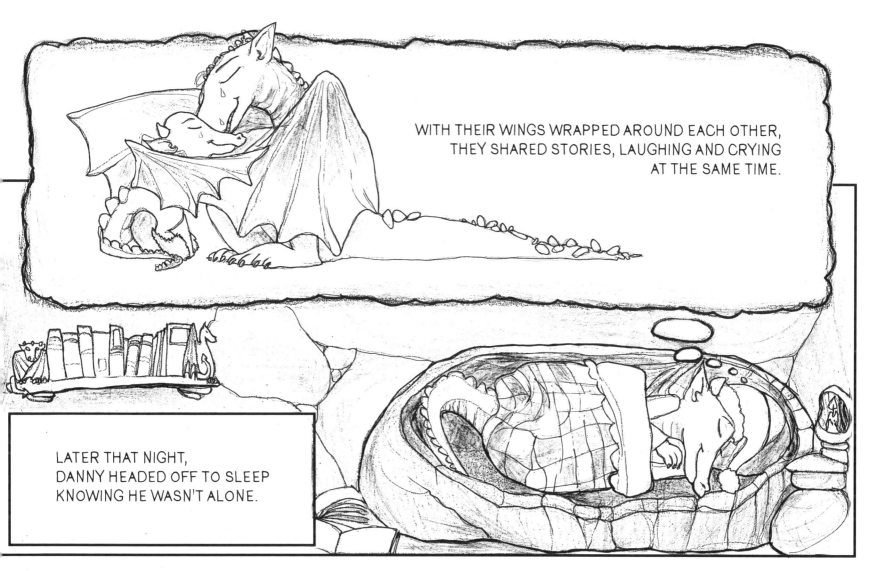

WITH THEIR WINGS WRAPPED AROUND EACH OTHER, THEY SHARED STORIES, LAUGHING AND CRYING AT THE SAME TIME.

LATER THAT NIGHT,
DANNY HEADED OFF TO SLEEP
KNOWING HE WASN'T ALONE.

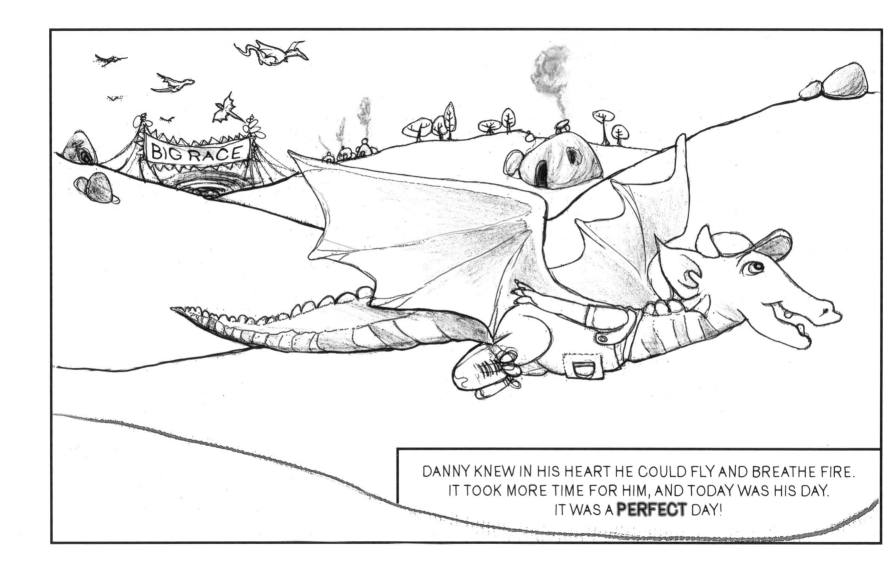

DANNY KNEW IN HIS HEART HE COULD FLY AND BREATHE FIRE.
IT TOOK MORE TIME FOR HIM, AND TODAY WAS HIS DAY.
IT WAS A **PERFECT** DAY!

FLYING HOME FROM THE BIG RACE,
DANNY STOPPED TO CHECK
THE MAILBOX ONCE MORE.
IN THE PILE OF LETTERS,
HE NOTICED ONE ADDRESSED TO HIM.

IT WAS FROM THE MASTER DRAGON.

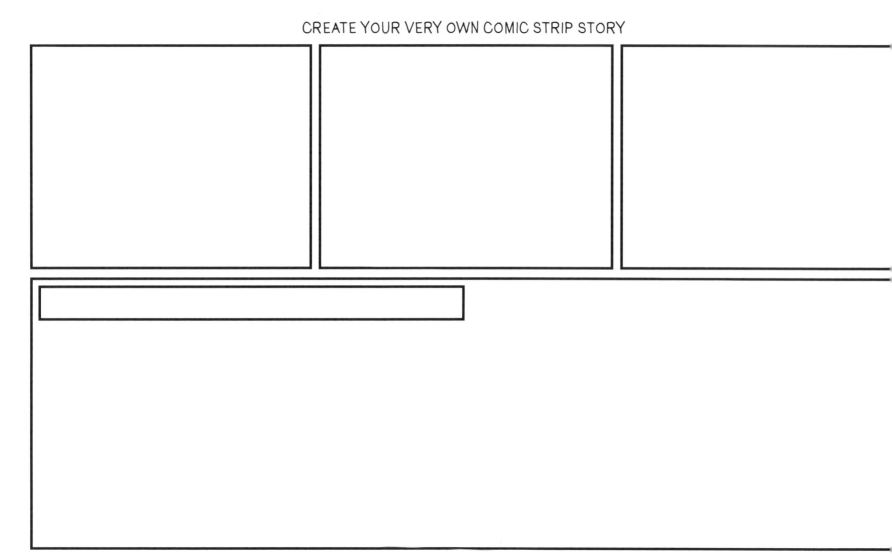

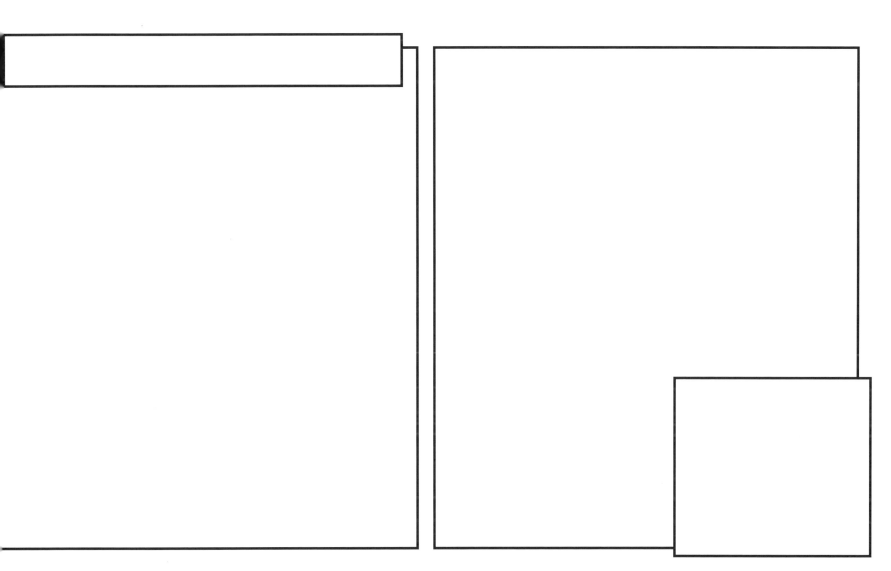

Alva Sachs earned her Bachelor of Science degree at the University of Illinois and her Master of Education degree from Northern Illinois University, and has more than sixteen years of teaching experience. Her life—long passion has been writing for children. Her days in the classroom provided the inspiration for becoming a children's writer. As the founder of Three Wishes Publishing Company, in 2007, she published *Circus Fever*, followed by *On Your Mark, Get Set, Go!* and *I'm 5*. Her books have received awards and honors in the picture book genre. Reading her stories in person at schools, libraries, book festivals, bookstores, and various venues has opened a whole new "classroom" for Alva. Her dedication to sharing the fun of reading has brought her a wonderful gift in return: creating stories that engage, excite, and empower the young reader. Serving as a Board Member of Reading Is Fundamental of Southern California, has provided Alva the opportunity to foster literacy by helping families to build home libraries. As a Board Member of the Angels of the Alliance, Alva works with the Thousand Oaks Civics Arts Plaza, whereby the Alliance for the Arts provides live theatre experiences for children of Title 1 schools to enhance their "Kids for the Arts," programming and funding. Alva has been recognized as one of the "50 Great Writers You Should Be Reading" in 2012—2013 by The Authors Show. Visit Alva at www.alvasachs.com.

Patricia Krebs is a multimedia artist who grew up in Buenos Aires, Argentina, where she obtained degrees in Fine Arts Education and in Contemporary Visual Arts. Her visual works have been exhibited in galleries and cultural centers throughout South and North America, and have been featured in books, CD covers, educational publications, and award winning children's picture books. In addition, she creates puppets, props and masks for theatrical events, and recently debuted as art director & production designer for stop—motion animation. Patricia is also a singer, writes songs for artists & videogame companies, and records Spanish voiceovers for films, such as *Harry Potter and the Goblet of Fire, Corpse Bride, Beowulf,* and *Happy Feet I & II*. Her published works have received special recognition from the Department of Cultural Affairs of Los Angeles *"in appreciation of outstanding and invaluable artistic contribution to the City of Los Angeles 2009 Latino Heritage Month"* and IBBY (International Board on Books for Young People). In 2012, Patricia received the Vision Award from the Reel Rasquache Arts & Film Festival in Los Angeles. To learn more about her, visit www.patriciakrebs.com.ar.